TIMMY TIGER
AND TOO MANY TWINS

Story by

Alvin M. Westcott

Illustrations by

Wallace Faucheux, Jr.

published by

ODDO PUBLISHING

Fayetteville, Georgia

Symbol for
exciting book ideas

Library of Congress Catalog Card Number 88-063238
ISBN 0-87783-251-X (Library Binding)
ISBN 0-87783-238-2 (Paperback)

Printed in the United States of America

It was a hot day in the jungle, and Timmy Tiger wanted to get cool.

"Mother, may I go swimming?" he asked.

"That is a good thing to do," Mother Tiger said. "Tommy can go, too."

"I want to go alone today," answered Timmy as he waved to his mother. "I'll be careful."

4

Soon Timmy met Edie and Eddie Elephant. "Hi, Tommy Tiger. Where is your brother Timmy?" they asked.

"I'm not Tommy. I'm Timmy! And I want to be alone today."

"You can't have much fun alone," said Edie.

"Yes I can!" Timmy shouted, and walked away.

High in a tree, Happy and Hoppy, the
Red Hornbills, called down, "Hello, Tommy
Tiger. Why are you alone today?"

Timmy started to answer, but did not. He
turned and ran to the pool, thinking all the way,
"I want to be me — Timmy!"

Everyone was having fun at the pool. Timmy
looked around. He saw twins everywhere. There
was Bubba and Bobo Water Buffalo, Fluffy and
8 Foo Foo Fox,

Tina and Gina Toddycat,

and Harry and Homer, the Hedgehog brothers.

10

Some yelled, "Hi, Tommy!" Some shouted, "Hello, Timmy!" They all asked, "Where is your brother?"

Timmy jumped up and down. "I'm not Tommy!
I'm TIMMY! Being a twin is no fun. Everyone
calls you the wrong name!"

12

"We are sorry, Timmy," said the Toddycat twins sadly. "Twins look the same. It is hard to tell who is who."

"I know me!" Timmy growled. "I have blue eyes. I don't like berries. Tommy has green eyes. He loves berries."

"Everyone confuses us, too," said Tina.

"Then you know how I feel, Tina. Or is it Gina?
I'm sorry. I do not know who is who." Timmy
shook his head.

"It's all right, Timmy. It's fun being the same!"
Both Toddycats smiled the same smile.

Timmy dived into the pool.

Harry and Homer Hedgehog asked Timmy to play catch. Back and forth they threw the ball. Then Timmy tossed the ball to Harry when it was Homer's turn to catch.

"I'm sorry. I cannot play anymore," cried Timmy. "I must be alone. There are too many twins here! There are too many twins everywhere!"

Off Timmy went into the jungle. He began to run. It felt good to run. Faster and faster he ran. He did not see the log. Whump! Over he went!

"OUCH!" cried Timmy. When he tried to walk he could not.

"How will I get home?" he thought. "It will be dark soon. Maybe it was not such a good idea to be alone. I wish Tommy was here now!"

Timmy yelled as loud as he could. "Help! Help!
Someone please help me!"
   Soon he heard leaves rustling and branches
cracking.

"Hooray!" Timmy shouted. "It's Tommy!
Over here, Tommy!"

But it was not Tommy! From under a bush
slithered Big Blacky Python, the jungle bully.
   "What a nic-c-c-ce fur coat you have, little tiger.
It will do nic-c-c-cely for my bed!" hissed the Python.
Closer and closer he inched toward Timmy.

Painfully, Timmy
crawled to a nearby cliff.
From his perch, he heard chattering.
It was the Chimp twins, Charlie and Champ.
"Help!" Timmy yelled. "Big Blacky is after me!
I'm hurt and cannot run! Please find my brother
Tommy. Tell him to come quick!"

"Don't worry, Timmy! We'll find Tommy!" the
Chimp twins shouted as they raced off through the
trees.

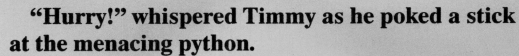

"Hurry!" whispered Timmy as he poked a stick at the menacing python.

"It's-s-s-s too late," hissed Big Blacky. "Your friends-s-s-s cannot s-s-s-save you!" The python's jaws opened wide.

Suddenly there was a loud...

CRASH! The startled python whirled.
Coming toward him was Tommy and all
the animal twins. Leading the charging
rescuers was Timmy's mother.

Mother Tiger gave a ferocious snarl.
"Leave Timmy alone!" she roared.

26

Big Blacky was so surprised he lost his balance. Over he rolled down a rocky hill and into a briar patch.

Mother Tiger snapped at his tail. Terrified,
the battered python raced quickly off into the
jungle.

"I'm safe!" cried Timmy. "Thank you all!"
Tommy and the Toddycat sisters found two
sticks for splints. Soon Mother Tiger had Timmy's
leg bandaged.

As the day turned to dusk, all the friends started home. Two by two they marched. Leading the parade rode Timmy on his mother's back.

"I guess being a twin isn't so bad," Timmy sighed.

Tommy nodded. "When there are two, you help me and I help you."

"Tommy's right," Mother Tiger assured Timmy. "You are very lucky to have a brother like Tommy. And you are lucky to have so many friends."

Timmy agreed. But for now, at least for a while,
everyone could tell who was Timmy and who was
Tommy. Tommy did all the helping. Timmy did all
the hopping.

Timmy was smiling again. He liked being a twin
after all.

about the author

ALVIN M. WESTCOTT is the author of many books and articles for and about children and their learning processes. Presently, Alvin M. Westcott is Associate Professor of Elementary Education at State University of New York at Oswego, N.Y. He earned his B.S. degree in Elementary Education at Oneonta, New York, and his M.S. degree at Syracuse University.

Professor Westcott's extensive background, both in and out of the field of education, combine superbly with his keen insight into children's likes and dislikes and his uncanny wit and humor. Through his talented pen he has helped open the wonderful world of reading to children.

Among the many books and articles written by Professor Westcott are several for Oddo Publishing, including *Rockets and Crackers*, *Fun With Timothy Triangle*, *Word Bending With Aunt Sarah*, *Billy Lump's Adventure*, and now, *Timmy Tiger and Too Many Twins*.

In his spare time, Alvin M. Westcott enjoys several hobbies. He is an accomplished painter, and has had his works displayed in many art exhibits. He also is an avid reader and stamp collector. The father of three children, Professor Westcott currently resides with two cats and many goldfish.

about the illustrator

WALLACE FAUCHEUX, JR., Wally as he prefers to be called, is a native of South Louisiana. He began his study of commercial art at Delgado Jr. College in New Orleans. His formal art education provided the basics. His style and technique are self-taught, born of his innate creativeness, his study of the animation works of Disney and Warner Brothers, and his observation of the world around him. In addition, he has been greatly influenced by the late John Chase, nationally known political cartoonist and native of New Orleans.

Presently Wally works as a graphics illustrator for CBS affiliate WWL TV in New Orleans, Louisiana. He is also a free-lance illustrator with his works commissioned by such well-known concerns as Tulane University, Popeye's Famous Fried Chicken & Biscuits, Union Carbide Corporation, Coca-Cola, The Louisiana Bar Association, Times Picayune States Item Newspaper, Child Care Review Magazine, and many others. Wally's versatility is evidenced by the wide variety of illustrations he has completed including program covers and posters for sporting events, magazine covers, editorial cartoons, audio-visual training books, and now, children's books.

Timmy Tiger and Too Many Twins is Wally's latest addition to the expanding array of his artistic accomplishments.